Neil Gaiman
Chu's Day
at the Beach

Illustrated By Adam Rex

For Eve Gonson, a perfect audience.
– N.G.

For Henry.
– A.R.

Bloomsbury Publishing, London, Oxford, New York, New Delhi and Sydney
First published in Great Britain in 2015 by Bloomsbury Publishing Plc
50 Bedford Square, London, WC1B 3DP

This paperback edition first published in Great Britain in 2016 by Bloomsbury Publishing Plc

First published in the US in 2015 by HarperCollins Children's Books, a division of
HarperCollins Publishers, 195 Broadway, New York, NY 10007

A CIP catalogue record of this book is available from the British Library

ISBN 978 1 4088 6435 7 (HB)
ISBN 978 1 4088 6436 4 (PB)
ISBN 978 1 4088 8048 7 (eBook)

Printed in China by Leo Paper Products, Heshan, Guangdong
13 5 7 9 10 8 6 4 2

All papers used by Bloomsbury Publishing are natural, recyclable products made from
wood grown in well managed forests. The manufacturing processes conform to
the environmental regulations of the country of origin

www.bloomsbury.com

BLOOMSBURY is a registered trademark of Bloomsbury Publishing Plc

When Chu sneezed,

big things happened.

It was a hot day, and Chu and his family went to the beach.

Chu had an ice cream. The ice-cream
seller was very nice. She gave Chu an
extra scoop of vanilla.

Chu said hello
to a crab in a rock pool.
Chu's mother sat on the sand
and read her book. Chu's father
went into the water up to
his tummy.

Chu took off his sunglasses. He looked at
the sea. The day was so sunny and bright.

Chu's nose tickled.

It was a tickling that got bigger and bigger and bigger.

It was a tickling that filled his whole head . . .

AAH-

AAAAH-

AAAAAH-

CHOOOOOOOO!

"Uh-oh,"
said Chu.

"Chu," said Chu's mother.

"Chu!" said
Chu's father.
"What did
you DO?"

All the people on the
beach went down to look.

Chu said hello to some fish. The
fish looked at him. They looked sad.

He waved at a family of merpandas. The littlest merpanda waved back at him.

Chu saw a whale.

The whale was very big.
"With the sea broken, I
cannot go home," said
the whale.

"You must put this back the way
it was," said the ice-cream seller.
"Or nobody will come
to the beach
any more, and
they will not
eat my
ice cream."

Please sneeze again, Chu.
But Chu could not sneeze.

A seagull tickled Chu's
nose with a feather.
"Will you sneeze?"
said the seagull.

AAH.

AAAAH.

AAAAAH.

"No," said Chu.

"Perhaps a bubbly drink will make you sneeze," said the ice-cream seller. She gave Chu a fizzy drink, with bubbles that went up Chu's nose.

Please sneeze again, Chu. Will you sneeze now?

AAH.

AAAAH.

AAAAAH.

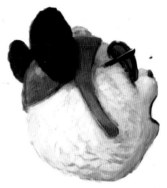

"No," said Chu.

All of the grown-ups were very sad.
"Chu will not sneeze," they said.
"Now the sea is broken and
we cannot fix it."

Then Tiny the snail climbed up to
Chu's ear and whispered, "Sometimes
I sneeze when I see the sun."

Chu took off his sunglasses.

AAAA

"There," said Chu. "Everything is back just as it was before."

The ice-cream seller was so pleased,
she gave Chu another ice cream.

In the sea, Chu saw a merpanda
just his size. She swam over to him.

"Sometimes I sneeze too," she said.
And then she swam away.

"Did you have a nice day at the beach?" asked Chu's mother and father.

"I had the best day at the beach," said Chu, holding his seagull feather.

Goodnight.